THE CROWS' NEST

For very dear Joan, with love – SAH

For my baby sister Alice – JT

First published in 2001 by Franklin Watts,
96 Leonard Street, London EC2A 4XD

Franklin Watts Australia
56 O'Riordan Street
Alexandria, NSW 2015

Text © 2001 Sandra Ann Horn
Illustrations © 2001 Joseph Theobald

ISBN 0 7496 3941 5 (hardback)
ISBN 0 7496 4242 4 (paperback)

A CIP catalogue record is available
from the British Library.
Dewey Classification 598.8

Printed in Hong Kong/China

THE CROWS' NEST

SANDRA ANN HORN • JOSEPH THEOBALD

W
FRANKLIN WATTS
LONDON•SYDNEY

Jo and Mo were sitting in a tall tree.
Handsome Jo blinked his bead-bright eyes.
Comely Mo preened her silken feathers.
They were looking for a home.

Down below, the farmer was
planting turnip seeds. He covered
the patch with twigs to keep
the hens off. Then he went indoors.

'Quawk!' said Mo, and 'Quark!' said Jo.
They gathered up all the twigs and
built themselves a fine nest.
    While they were busy in the tree,
the hens were busy in the turnip patch.
They scratched up the seeds and
ate them, every one.

The farmer ran out. He jumped
up and down and waved a big
stick at Mo and Jo.
   'Dratted crows!' he shouted.
   'Quah?' said Mo. 'Cor!' said Jo.
They flew off out of harm's way.
   It was no place for crows.

Mo and Jo flew far away from
the farm, looking and looking.
By and by, they came to a row
of trees, with short flat branches.
'Quar?' said Jo. 'Cark!' said Mo.

They gathered twigs for a new nest.
Jo found a good long one in a puddle.
He dropped the wet twig on to the
nest. There was a loud bang and a
shower of sparks. All the lights went
out for miles around.

'Wau-aaaghh!' Jo and Mo flew for
their lives. It was no place for crows.

At last, weary Mo and tired Jo found a tall pointed tree and, once again, began to gather twigs. There was Sunday-morning quiet all around. Then below them, a rope swung. There was a terrible noise.

'Boi-oi-oing! Boi-oi-oing!!'

The nest swung up, and all the twigs went clattering down. Mo and Jo flapped up into the air and away. It was no place for crows.

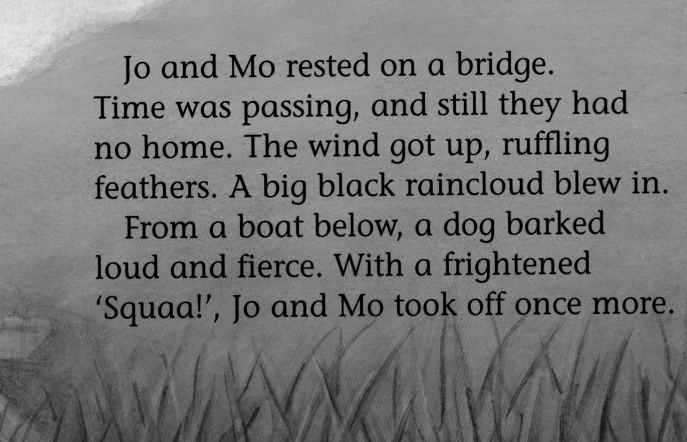

Jo and Mo rested on a bridge.
Time was passing, and still they had
no home. The wind got up, ruffling
feathers. A big black raincloud blew in.
From a boat below, a dog barked
loud and fierce. With a frightened
'Squaa!', Jo and Mo took off once more.

On and on the crows flew.
There was nowhere to rest.
There was nowhere
to build a home.

Still they flew on
through the storm and
the dark, until they were
as weary as crows can be.
'Cwer! Cwer! Cwer!'
the crows called to each other,
but the wind blew their cries away.

When Jo was almost flying in his sleep
and Mo could scarcely flap her wings,
they came to a forest of very tall trees.
'Quee?' said Mo.
'Quoh!' said Jo.

Mo and Jo chose a fine tall tree.
There were lots of twigs all around.
Some were strange shapes, but it didn't
matter. They built a beautiful nest and
lined it with soft pink moss.

'Look what the clever crows have made,' said the other tree-dwellers.
'Isn't he handsome! Isn't she comely!'
'Quark! Quark!' called happy Mo and proud Jo.

On the ground, under bright bushes, there was food a-plenty. Mo and Jo grew sleek and plump. By and by, Mo laid five pale eggs in the splendid nest.

Soon there were five downy crowlets,
with yellow beaks open wide.
    'Look at the dear little babies!'
said the other tree-dwellers.
They put special titbits out for
Mo and Jo and the crowlets.
    'After all,' they said,
'we're neighbours.'

'Querdle-erdle-oo!'
sang Mo and Jo.
Here was a place for crows.